WITHDRAWN

A Visit To GRANDMA'S

Nancy Carlson

Viking

VIKING
Published by the Penguin Group
Viking Penguin, a division of Penguin Books USA Inc.,
375 Hudson Street, New York, New York 10014, U.S.A.
Penguin Books Ltd, 27 Wrights Lane, London W8 5TZ, England
Penguin Books Australia Ltd, Ringwood, Victoria, Australia
Penguin Books Canada Ltd, 2801 John Street, Markham, Ontario, Canada L3R 1B4
Penguin Books (N.Z.) Ltd, 182–190 Wairau Road, Auckland 10, New Zealand

Penguin Books Ltd, Registered Offices: Harmondsworth, Middlesex, England

First published in 1991 by Viking Penguin, a division of Penguin Books USA Inc.

1   3   5   7   9   10   8   6   4   2

Library of Congress Cataloging-in-Publication Data
Carlson, Nancy.
A visit to grandma's / by Nancy Carlson.   p.   cm.
Summary: Tina and her parents visit Grandma in her new Florida
condominium and are surprised to find that she is very
different from when she lived on the farm.
ISBN 0-670-83288-X
[1. Grandmothers—Fiction.]   I. Title.
P27.C21664VI   1991   [E]—dc20
91-2739   CIP   AC

Printed in Hong Kong
Set in 16 pt. Weidemann

Florida

S

Pensacola

Tallahassee

Jacksonville

ORLANDO "FUN"

TAMPA

St. Petersburg

Pompano

Fort Lauderdale

Miami

Everglades

**Dedicated to
Grandpa John
who loved
warm weather**

Tina and her parents were going to fly to Florida to visit her grandmother in her new home for Thanksgiving.

"I'll sure miss the old farm," said Dad,
"but I can't wait to see Grandma."

"Ahh—I can almost smell Grandma's pumpkin pies," said Dad.
"I can almost taste her turkey and stuffing," said Tina.

Tina, Mom, and Dad couldn't believe
their eyes when they saw Grandma.

"Is that you, Grandma?" asked Tina.
"Are you okay?" said Dad.

"I feel great!
Hop in!!!" said Grandma.

When they got to Grandma's condo,
it wasn't at all like the old farm.

"Well, I suppose you'll start baking pies now!" said Dad.
"No time! I'll pick some up at the store
after aerobics," said Grandma.

"Store-bought pies! Grandma has always baked her own pies," complained Dad.

After her aerobics class, Grandma invited her
friends Bill, Dottie, Vernice, and Dorothy over.

They played charades until midnight!

On Thanksgiving morning, Grandma got up to go to tap-dance class.
"Aren't we having your famous cinnamon rolls?" said Mom.
"Goodness' sakes, no! That's not good for you. There are health shakes
 in the fridge," said Grandma.

"Grandma has changed," said Mom.
"I hope she's home in time to make
turkey dinner," said Tina.

When Grandma got home, she told them they were
meeting friends at Monti's Fish and Chips.

"What, no turkey dinner? I want Thanksgiving
like it always was," said Tina.

But Monti's was great!

Tina discovered she loved stone crab.

All during dinner, Bill pulled quarters out of
Tina's ears. Vernice told funny stories,

and Dottie had a purse full of candy.

After dinner, they all went to the condo for pie.
"I must say, this pie isn't as good as mine," said Grandma.

"I like it better,"
Dad whispered to Tina.

"Remember at the farm we used to take a
sleigh ride after dinner?" said Tina.

"Well, we can't take a sleigh, but we can
take a ride! Let's go!" said Grandma.

"This is fun!" said Tina.

When it was time to go home, Tina, Mom, and
Dad agreed it had been a great Thanksgiving.
"We'll be back in the spring," said Mom.

"Be sure to make reservations at Monti's!" said Tina.
"And don't forget to buy those good pies!" said Dad.